Sue's Supermarket Dash

T0321623

Written by Hannah Fish
Illustrated by Lee Teng

Collins

Who's in this story?

Listen and say

Daddy

Download the audio at www.collins.co.uk/839712

Mummy

Sue

Sue is at the supermarket.
Sue says, "I would like some cheese, please."
The woman can't see Sue.

Sue says, "Put it in the trolley, please."

7

Sue says, "Thank you. My mummy LOVES bananas."

9

Sue sees the cakes. They are beautiful. Sue likes cakes. She looks on her shopping list.

Hmmm ....
Cake ...
Mummy likes cake.

Sue says, "One chocolate cake and one fruit cake, please."

13

Sue is looking at the flowers.

Sue says, "Oh no! Mummy likes these flowers."

Daddy says, "There you are. Are you OK, Sue?"

Sue says, "No! There are no flowers for Mummy."

A girl says, "Hello."

Sue says, "Don't worry, Daddy.
This is all for Mummy."

Sue says, "Let's go, Daddy!"

Sue says, "Happy Mother's Day, Mummy!"

Mummy says, "Wow! Bananas, cheese, cakes, sweets AND beautiful flowers."

Picture dictionary

Listen and repeat

bananas

cake

cheese

flowers

supermarket

sweets

trolley

1 Look and order the story

2 Listen and say

Collins

Published by Collins
An imprint of HarperCollins*Publishers*
Westerhill Road
Bishopbriggs
Glasgow
G64 2QT

HarperCollins*Publishers*
1st Floor, Watermarque Building
Ringsend Road
Dublin 4
Ireland

William Collins' dream of knowledge for all began with the publication of his first book in 1819.

A self-educated mill worker, he not only enriched millions of lives, but also founded a flourishing publishing house. Today, staying true to this spirit, Collins books are packed with inspiration, innovation and practical expertise. They place you at the centre of a world of possibility and give you exactly what you need to explore it.

© HarperCollins*Publishers* Limited 2020

10 9 8 7 6 5 4 3 2

ISBN 978-0-00-839712-8

Collins® and COBUILD® are registered trademarks of HarperCollins*Publishers* Limited

www.collins.co.uk/elt

British Library Cataloguing in Publication Data

A catalogue record for this publication is available from the British Library.

Author: Hannah Fish
Illustrator: Lee Teng (Beehive)
Series editor: Rebecca Adlard
Publishing manager: Lisa Todd
Product managers: Jennifer Hall and Caroline Green
In-house editor: Alma Puts Keren
Project manager: Emily Hooton
Editor: Tessie Papadopoulou-Dalton
Proofreaders: Natalie Murray and Michael Lamb
Cover designer: Kevin Robbins
Typesetter: 2Hoots Publishing Services Ltd
Audio produced by id audio, London
Reading guide author: Emma Wilkinson
Production controller: Rachel Weaver
Printed and bound by: GPS Group, Slovenia

Download the audio for this book and a reading guide for parents and teachers at www.collins.co.uk/839712